Dogs

D0708602

INTRODUCTION

It is generally agreed nowadays that the many different breeds of dog are all descended from that great wild dog, the wolf. If you have ever watched the behaviour of wild wolves on wildlife films or even in zoos, you will realise that our cuddly household pets have many similar characteristics. Over the years, humans learned to breed dogs to carry out particular tasks. Some had strong herding instincts – and these became the shepherd dogs we know so well today.

Others were just good companions and became 'man's best friend'. Taking on a dog is a great responsibility and should not be taken lightly. Dogs do not just need feeding – they require regular exercise (some need a great deal) to ensure their wellbeing. Many have coats that require a lot of care and most importantly, in order to be happy they need lots of loving attention. Remember that the character of the dog as described in this book should only be taken as a guide. Like all animals, including people, each dog is an individual with its own personality and temperament.

Again, like people, a dog's character will be influenced by its environment. Also, female dogs may behave differently than male dogs of the same breed. A dog is a long term commitment but if you give your pet the care and attention it deserves, owning a dog is a very rewarding experience.

How to use your i-SPY book

The breeds of dog in this book have been arranged in groups according to their original function – Gundog, Hound, Pastoral, Terrier, Toy, Utility and Working – and within each group they are arranged alphabetically. You need 1000 points to send off for your i-SPY certificate (see page 64) but that is not too difficult because there are masses of points in every book. Each entry has a star or circle and points value beside it. The stars represent harder to spot entries. As you make each i-SPY, write your score in the circle or star.

Points: 15

BRITTANY

Size Medium
Walks More than two hours a day
Grooming More than once a week

A busy dog, he is affectionate and has a pleasant nature. Easy to train, his dense, fine coat is not difficult to keep clean.

ENGLISH SETTER

Top Spot!   Points: 20

Size Large
Walks More than two hours a day
Grooming More than once a week

One of the most glamorous of all breeds, they make great working dogs as well as lovable companions.

GERMAN POINTER (SHORT-HAIRED)

Points: 5

Size Large
Walks More than two hours a day
Grooming Once a week

He is a highly trainable and very friendly dog. He shows real grace and is a pleasure to watch, but you will get tired before he will!

GERMAN POINTER
(WIRE-HAIRED)

Size Large
Walks More than two hours a day
Grooming More than once a week

Easily trained and friendly, he has a tough, cheerful appearance, making him both a good family dog and worker.

Points: 10

GORDON SETTER

Size Large
Walks More than two hours a day
Grooming More than once a week

He is trainable and an intelligent dog capable of enjoying all the exercise an owner can give him.

Points: 10

Points: 5

HUNGARIAN VIZSLA

Size Large
Walks More than two hours a day
Grooming Once a week

Being an intelligent, friendly dog, with a good memory, he is easy to train. He is a very popular pet in his native Hungary and can adapt to homes of all sizes.

Vizslas are a very old breed, with the first written reference about them appearing in the 14th century.

HUNGARIAN VIZSLA (WIRE-HAIRED)

Points: 10

Size Large
Walks More than two hours a day
Grooming More than once a week

With a harsh wiry coat and bushy eyebrows he can sometimes look a little bit stern but has the same friendly character as his smooth-coated cousin.

For simplicity of reference it is common to use the male reference when referring to dogs.

IRISH RED AND WHITE SETTER

Top Spot!   Points: 20

Size Large
Walks More than two hours a day
Grooming More than once a week

He is a good-natured dog who is happy to join in family activities – and he really enjoys his food! He has lots of energy, and once fully grown, he needs lots of space to run around.

Points: 10 — IRISH SETTER

Size Large
Walks More than two hours a day
Grooming More than once a week

His happy-go-lucky attitude is very endearing and his friendly, affectionate nature makes him a good household dog ready for all the fun and games a family will provide.

ITALIAN SPINONE — Points: 10

Size Large
Walks More than two hours a day
Grooming More than once a week

An easy dog to train, he will fit into the family environment. His thick and wiry coat is simple to keep in good condition and its texture means that he does not bring too much dirt into the house after a muddy walk.

Points: 10 — POINTER

Size Medium
Walks More than two hours a day
Grooming Once a week

A neat looking dog with a very even temper. He is capable of fitting into a family but he is most at home out hunting on the moors.

i *Pointers get their names from the fact that when out hunting on the moors, they alert their handler to hiding birds by literally pointing to them with their nose.*

RETRIEVER (CHESAPEAKE BAY)

Points: 15

Size Large
Walks More than two hours a day
Grooming Once a week

Unfailing courage, endless energy, muscle power, a love of food and affection with a touch of independence, all go to produce a dog for the energetic family.

RETRIEVER (CURLY-COATED)

Size Large
Walks More than two hours a day
Grooming More than once a week

His waterproof coat is well designed for his love of the outdoors; even after a swim, all it takes is a few quick shakes and he is practically dry. But his unique tightly curled coat does require special care to keep it at its best.

Points: 25 **Top Spot!**

RETRIEVER (FLAT-COATED)

Size Large
Walks More than two hours a day
Grooming More than once a week

He is a slow-maturing dog, who keeps his delightful puppy-like qualities for several years. He is outgoing and eager to please.

Points: 5

5 Points: 5

RETRIEVER (GOLDEN)

Size Large
Walks More than two hours a day
Grooming More than once a week

Goldens are easy to train, rarely fussy eaters and have a thick coat that is reasonably easy to keep clean. It is no surprise that the breed has become one of the most popular dogs.

(i) *In 2006 there was a gathering of Golden Retrievers in Scotland (their original home) where a record-breaking photograph was taken of 188 Goldens in one image.*

RETRIEVER (LABRADOR)

Points: 5 **5**

Size Large
Walks More than two hours a day
Grooming Once a week

A real gentleman, he adores children and has a kind and loving nature and a confident air. City living is not really his scene – he is more at home in the countryside.

(i) *Labradors have webbed toes, a thick otter-like tail and dense coats making them fantastic swimmers in even the coldest of water.*

RETRIEVER (NOVA SCOTIA DUCK TOLLING)

Points: 10

Size Medium
Walks Up to one hour a day
Grooming More than once a week

A handsome dog who makes an ideal and enthusiastic family companion for the active household. He enjoys dog sports such as agility and frisbee, and is easy to groom.

SPANIEL (AMERICAN COCKER)

Size Medium
Walks More than two hours a day
Grooming Every day

He has a cheerful nature and makes a highly successful family dog. Being compact, he doesn't eat much but he does need careful grooming.

Points: 10

SPANIEL (CLUMBER)

Size Large
Walks Up to one hour a day
Grooming More than once a week

A well-mannered companion who is lovely to have around. He truly deserves greater popularity as he fits in well to family life.

Points: 20 Top Spot!

Points: 5

SPANIEL (COCKER)

Size Medium
Walks Up to one hour a day
Grooming Every day

A busy little dog who enjoys plenty of exercise, thrives on human companionship and can often be found with a toy or slipper in his mouth, with his tail wagging furiously.

The name 'cocker' is derived from the fact that these dogs were originally bred to disturb Woodcock for shooting.

SPANIEL (ENGLISH SPRINGER)

Points: 5

Size Medium
Walks More than two hours a day
Grooming More than once a week

Like so many of the gundog breeds, his cheerful outgoing nature makes him endearing and he is a popular choice as an energetic family companion.

In 1982 Bob, an English Springer Spaniel, owned by Lord David Sutch (Screaming Lord Sutch) stood for Parliament representing 'The Monster Raving Loony Barking Mad Dog Party'.

Points: 25 Top Spot!

SPANIEL (FIELD)

Size Medium
Walks More than two hours a day
Grooming More than once a week

This breed is most definitely not suited to city living – but he makes an excellent companion for people who prefer rural life.

SPANIEL (IRISH WATER)

Size Large
Walks More than two hours a day
Grooming More than once a week

He is by nature a very affectionate dog and has a distinct sense of humour. He is not a big eater for his size, and makes a lovable family dog who is never one to say no to a walk!

SPANIEL (SUSSEX)

Size Medium
Walks More than two hours a day
Grooming More than once a week

His rather wrinkled brows can give him a frowning look but that is as far as the frown goes; he is a kind dog capable of being an excellent family dog in a country household.

Points: 25 Top Spot!

Points: 25 Top Spot!

Points: 10

SPANIEL (WELSH SPRINGER)

Size Medium
Walks More than two hours a day
Grooming More than once a week

The Welsh is somewhat smaller than the English Springer. He is also easier to keep clean in wet weather – and his temperament is just as kind.

WEIMARANER

Points: 5

Size Large
Walks More than two hours a day
Grooming Once a week

With a silvery-grey coat and his light-coloured eyes, the Weimaraner has increased in popularity and has found a lot of friends as a companion dog.

Weimaraner puppies are born with stripes which last until they are a few days old.

AFGHAN HOUND

Points: 15

Size Large
Walks More than two hours a day
Grooming Every day

Afghans have a tendency to be shy with strangers, but they are very affectionate and are faithful to their owner.

Points: 20   **Top Spot!**

BASENJI

Size Small
Walks Up to one hour a day
Grooming Once a week

He is curious, self-confident and friendly, and becomes very attached to his human family. He loves to play but don't leave belongings lying around as he likes to chew!

 Basenjis are known as the 'barkless dog' – a unique characteristic of the breed – and show happiness with a crowing-yodelling noise.

Points: 15

BASSET GRIFFON VENDEEN (GRAND)

Size Medium
Walks More than two hours a day
Grooming Every day

This is a dog with a sense of humour who loves to join in human activity. Being a true hound he has a tendency to be hard of hearing when it suits him and is notorious for escaping!

BASSET GRIFFON VENDEEN (PETIT)

Size Medium
Walks Up to one hour a day
Grooming More than once a week

A typical hound, his happy, extrovert temperament helps make him a breed for the healthy, fun-loving family.

Points: 15

BASSET HOUND

Size Large
Walks Up to one hour a day
Grooming Once a week

He is often portrayed by cartoonists as a kindly but worried canine buffoon but the Basset deserves his popularity as a family dog; he is as happy curled up by the fire as he is romping in the garden.

Points: 10

BEAGLE

Points: 5

Size Medium
Walks More than two hours a day
Grooming Once a week

He makes a first-class family pet – a bustling, eager little dog, full of enthusiasm and energy, ever ready for any activity that involves him.

The Peanuts character 'Snoopy' is often described as the world's most famous Beagle.

Points: 15

BLOODHOUND

Size Large
Walks More than two hours a day
Grooming Once a week

He is generally good-natured and affectionate but can be a bit sensitive. He has a deep loud voice that cannot be ignored.

His amazing ability to follow a human scent over all types of terrain for many hours has given the Bloodhound an almost super-canine reputation, which has been promoted by writers of detective fiction.

Points: 15

BORZOI

Size Large
Walks Up to one hour a day
Grooming More than once a week

The elegant, gentle Borzoi is laid-back and happy to relax with familiar people but can be sensitive to their surroundings and wary of strangers.

DACHSHUND
(LONG-HAIRED)

Size Medium
Walks Up to one hour a day
Grooming More than once a week

Dachshunds are active dogs and once fully mature, will take as much exercise as you can give them; you are likely to want to go home before they do!

Points: 15

DACHSHUND
(MINIATURE LONG-HAIRED)

Size Small
Walks Up to 30 minutes a day
Grooming More than once a week

Dachshunds are perfectly happy curled up on your lap snoozing. They are loyal companions and generally make good family pets.

Points: 10

DACHSHUND (MINIATURE SMOOTH-HAIRED)

Points: 5

Size Small
Walks Up to 30 minutes a day
Grooming Once a week

Dachshunds are not noted for their obedience but with patience and persistence they can be trained very well.

DACHSHUND
(MINIATURE WIRE-HAIRED)

Size Small
Walks Up to 30 minutes a day
Grooming More than once a week

Dachshunds are most definitely small hounds and when they catch a scent they can 'go deaf' if it suits them!

Points: 10

DACHSHUND
(SMOOTH-HAIRED)

Size Medium
Walks Up to one hour a day
Grooming Once a week

Their bark can be deep and people are often surprised to hear such a deep noise coming from a dog the size of a Dachshund.

Points: 10

Points: 10

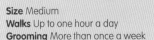

DACHSHUND (WIRE-HAIRED)

Size Medium
Walks Up to one hour a day
Grooming More than once a week

Dachshunds are scrappy little dogs that will gladly choose the role of a security guard and will send any unwelcome guests packing!

i *The name 'Dachshund' roughly translates as 'badger dog', as they were once used for hunting badgers. The smaller miniature varieties were more commonly used for hunting foxes and rabbits. They are the only breed of dog that will hunt both above and below the ground.*

DEERHOUND

Top Spot! **Points: 20**

Size Giant
Walks More than two hours a day
Grooming More than once a week

Dignity, humour, affection and loyalty all play their part in the temperament of this sensitive soul. But his true passion is for exercise – and plenty of it!

FOXHOUND

Top Spot!   **Points: 20**

Size Large
Walks More than two hours a day
Grooming Once a week

As they were bred to live in packs, Foxhounds are happiest in the company of other dogs. They have to investigate everything and anything – often with little thought for any furniture that may be in the way!

ⓘ *Foxhounds were originally bred to hunt foxes in a pack with huntsmen on horseback.*

Points: 20   **Top Spot!**

GREYHOUND

Size Large
Walks Up to one hour a day
Grooming Once a week

These gentle dogs are happy to lie around all day (on the sofa - not the floor!) and make calm and gentle companions, but they must be thoroughly exercised.

ⓘ *Despite there being thousands of racing Greyhounds, this breed is becoming very rare as there are few Greyhound breeders breeding for dog shows or domestic homes.*

Points: 10

IRISH WOLFHOUND

Size Giant
Walks More than two hours a day
Grooming More than once a week

In spite of his size, he is one of the gentlest of dogs with a proud yet calm expression, but his dark eyes can sometimes light up with a flash of mischief!

OTTERHOUND

Size Large
Walks More than two hours a day
Grooming More than once a week

He is a kind fellow with a typical loud baying call. A dog for the energetic but not for the house-proud!

Points: 25 Top Spot!

RHODESIAN RIDGEBACK

Size Large
Walks More than two hours a day
Grooming Once a week

He is an excellent family dog, good with children, affectionate and very loyal and protective of his family.

Points: 5

SALUKI

Points: 15

Size Large
Walks More than two hours a day
Grooming Once a week

He is highly strung, very sensitive, very intelligent and extremely affectionate to those he loves. He is a great running companion – if you can keep up with him!

 Points: 5

WHIPPET

Size Medium
Walks Up to one hour a day
Grooming Once a week

'Gentle' and 'affectionate' are somewhat of an understatement – he loves the company of people and is equally at home in castle or cottage.

i *It is thought that the name 'Whippet' comes from their quick movement and sharp nature – being like a 'little whip'.*

Points: 15

AUSTRALIAN CATTLE DOG

Size Medium
Walks Up to one hour a day
Grooming Once a week

This dog has great stamina and although wary of strangers, he is protective of his family and makes a dutiful companion.

AUSTRALIAN SHEPHERD

Size Medium
Walks More than two hours a day
Grooming More than once a week

He is intelligent and energetic but his territorial nature means his owner must be willing to provide him with the training and exercise he needs.

Points: 15

BEARDED COLLIE

Size Large
Walks Up to one hour a day
Grooming Every day

He is an active dog with a happy, outgoing nature – always ready for the next adventure!

Points: 10

BELGIAN SHEPHERD DOG (GROENENDAEL)   Points: 15

Size Medium
Walks More than two hours a day
Grooming More than once a week

Belgian Shepherds are an active and intelligent breed. They are playful and love to chase but they need plenty of exercise to keep them happy.

BELGIAN SHEPHERD DOG (LAEKENOIS)

Size Medium
Walks More than two hours a day
Grooming More than once a week

Belgian Shepherds are not well suited to city-living; they are happiest in a rural setting and with 'work' to do – be that herding or learning new tricks!

Points: 20   Top Spot!

BELGIAN SHEPHERD DOG (MALINOIS)

Size Medium
Walks More than two hours a day
Grooming More than once a week

Belgian Shepherds are loyal and affectionate to their owners but can be wary of new people.

Points: 15

BELGIAN SHEPHERD DOG (TERVUEREN)

Points: 20   Top Spot!

20

Size Medium
Walks More than two hours a day
Grooming More than once a week

Owing to their intelligence, Belgian Shepherds need a lot of physical and mental stimulation to keep them happy. They were originally bred for herding, so don't be surprised to see them trying to herd cyclists or joggers when out for a walk!

BORDER COLLIE

Points: 5

Size Medium
Walks More than two hours a day
Grooming More than once a week

He needs a lot of exercise, thrives on company and will always join in games. Dedicated to his family, he needs to work to be happy and is not content unless he is busy.

One of the most famous Border Collies in the UK was the Blue Peter dog 'Shep'. Shep's boisterous and excitable nature lead to the catchphrase 'Down Shep!' when trying to keep him under control.

Points: 15

BRIARD

Size Large
Walks More than two hours a day
Grooming Every day

Blessed with a fearless temperament, he makes a good family dog. He is an extrovert who loves to engage in games.

COLLIE (ROUGH)

Points: 5

Size Large
Walks Up to one hour a day
Grooming Every day

This breed is more than just a pretty face – they were bred to work, and their strong herding instinct is still apparent today.

This breed cannot be referred to without mentioning the most famous Rough Collie of all – Lassie! Lassie was so famous in the 1950s, 1960s and 1970s, that even today dogs of this breed are referred to as 'Lassie dogs'.

Points: 25 Top Spot!

COLLIE (SMOOTH)

Size Large
Walks Up to one hour a day
Grooming Once a week

This breed can be sensitive and reserved but he is gentle, affectionate and responsive to his owners.

FINNISH LAPPHUND

Size Medium
Walks Up to one hour a day
Grooming Every day

This breed is easy going and loves to please his owners in whatever activity he does. He is gentle and enjoys the company of children.

 Points: 15

GERMAN SHEPHERD DOG

Size Large
Walks More than two hours a day
Grooming More than once a week

He is a very intelligent breed and needs to be kept busy – if not he is likely to become bored and mischievous!

Points: 5

LANCASHIRE HEELER

Top Spot!   **Points: 20**

20

Size Small
Walks Up to one hour a day
Grooming Once a week

The Heeler is intelligent and eager-to-please with a love of people; he enjoys being with children and especially likes joining in games.

10   **Points: 10**

OLD ENGLISH SHEEPDOG

Size Large
Walks More than two hours a day
Grooming Every day

Intelligent and friendly, he is protective of his family and friends and has a particularly loud bark, which is likely to warn off any intruders!

i *The most famous Old English is the iconic Dulux dog. All the dogs (except one) used in the adverts have been champions – no fewer than five of them have been prize winners at Crufts!*

Points: 15

PYRENEAN MOUNTAIN DOG

Size Giant
Walks More than two hours a day
Grooming More than once a week

Once used as a guard dog, he has a very gentle side to his nature and is affectionate and tolerant with children, making him a popular house pet.

SAMOYED

Size Medium
Walks More than two hours a day
Grooming Every day

A true Sam is a friendly, positive, happy breed which explains why he has earned the nickname 'smiley dog'.

 Points: 10

SHETLAND SHEEPDOG

Size Small
Walks Up to one hour a day
Grooming Every day

This tireless and cheerful little dog always has to be 'on-the-go'. He is affectionate with his owner but a little reserved with strangers.

Points: 5

WELSH CORGI (CARDIGAN)

Top Spot! Points: 20

Size Medium
Walks Up to one hour a day
Grooming More than once a week

He gives the impression of being a restful character but is perfectly capable of becoming lively whenever he is asked to!

Points: 10

WELSH CORGI (PEMBROKE)

Size Medium
Walks Up to one hour a day
Grooming More than once a week

He has a bark which is much bigger than his small size would suggest and can be prone to eating much more than is good for him!

Points: 10

AIREDALE TERRIER

Size Large
Walks Up to one hour a day
Grooming Every day

An excellent family dog, particularly good with children and always ready to join in their games.

BEDLINGTON TERRIER

Size Medium
Walks Up to one hour a day
Grooming More than once a week

Despite appearances, he is a tough little dog, good in the house and makes a delightful family pet.

Points: 10

BORDER TERRIER

Size Small
Walks Up to one hour a day
Grooming More than once a week

Basically a worker but perfectly capable of being an active member of a family, having a temperament that combines good nature with a terrier's plucky spirit.

Points: 5

BULL TERRIER

Points: 5 5

Size Medium
Walks Up to one hour a day
Grooming Once a week

For all his somewhat standoffish appearance, he is in fact a very friendly dog who loves human company, even if he is prone to taking issue with the dog next door!

20 **Points: 20** **Top Spot!**

BULL TERRIER (MINIATURE)

Size Medium
Walks Up to one hour a day
Grooming Once a week

They love their family and are playful, determined and feisty!

ℹ️ *Bill Sykes's dog 'Bullseye' in the Charles Dickens novel 'Oliver Twist' was supposedly a Bull Terrier.*

5 Points: 5

CAIRN TERRIER

Size Small
Walks Up to one hour a day
Grooming Once a week

He loves people, is an able swimmer and a great hunter. Ready for any activity, he makes an ideal companion for a family, fitting in well with any lifestyle.

DANDIE DINMONT TERRIER

Size Medium
Walks Up to one hour a day
Grooming More than once a week

An intelligent chap with a will of his own – not the most obedient of pets! Devoted to children, he can melt the hardest of hearts with his soulful expression and laps up attention.

Points: 20 **Top Spot!**

FOX TERRIER
(SMOOTH)

Size Medium
Walks Up to one hour a day
Grooming Once a week

He is not the dog to let loose on a hillside covered with sheep but is ideally suited to family life in town or, if he is properly controlled, the country.

Points: 20 **Top Spot!**

FOX TERRIER (WIRE)

Points: 10

Size Medium
Walks Up to one hour a day
Grooming More than once a week

He is alert, very active, bold and is certainly not afraid to speak up for himself! Cheerful and happy, he makes an excellent children's playmate and family pet.

GLEN OF IMAAL TERRIER

Size Medium
Walks Up to one hour a day
Grooming More than once a week

He appears to be rather rough, but he is in fact a gentle family companion, not nearly as noisy as many small terriers – although he does have a deep bark!

Points: 25 Top Spot!

IRISH TERRIER

Size Medium
Walks Up to one hour a day
Grooming More than once a week

A daredevil at heart, the Irish Terrier nevertheless has the softest, most gentle and loving character, coupled with a delightful sense of humour.

Points: 20 Top Spot!

Points: 20   Top Spot!

KERRY BLUE TERRIER

Size Medium
Walks Up to one hour a day
Grooming Every day

An extrovert at heart, the Kerry is a compact, spirited dog, determined but adaptable. He makes a good house pet, kind with people but an excellent guard.

LAKELAND TERRIER

Top Spot!   Points: 20

Size Medium
Walks Up to one hour a day
Grooming More than once a week

A cheerful little rascal, he is hardy and agile as well as courageous, affectionate, tireless, lovable and naughty!

Points: 20   Top Spot!

MANCHESTER TERRIER

Size Small
Walks Up to one hour a day
Grooming Once a week

He makes a great companion, very agile and not aggressive. He becomes devoted to his family and fits into any environment, be it town or country.

NORFOLK TERRIER

Size Small
Walks Up to one hour a day
Grooming More than once a week

He has a delightful personality and although totally fearless, is not one to normally start a fight.

Points: 10

NORWICH TERRIER

Size Small
Walks Up to one hour a day
Grooming More than once a week

This breed are feisty little hunters, good watchdogs, responsive and loyal to their owners and usually friendly with strangers and other dogs.

Points: 20   Top Spot!

Points: 10

PARSON RUSSELL TERRIER

Size Medium
Walks Up to one hour a day
Grooming Once a week

He is best suited to country life and is too intelligent to be left on his own for long periods; he will get bored and could easily become destructive as well as noisy!

SCOTTISH TERRIER

Points: 10

Size Medium
Walks Up to one hour a day
Grooming Once a week

His public image is often that of a serious 'Scottie' but to his family and friends he is affectionate and cheerful, happy to curl up in a favourite armchair.

 The Scottie called 'Fala' who was owned by former US President Franklin D. Roosevelt is the only dog to ever be portrayed in a presidential memorial. The President reportedly never went anywhere without her.

SEALYHAM TERRIER

Top Spot! **Points: 25** 25

Size Medium
Walks Up to one hour a day
Grooming Every day

Fit, active and ready to frolic and play, he makes an intelligent and charming companion, happy to be with you or able to occupy himself, whichever the situation demands.

SOFT-COATED WHEATEN TERRIER

Size Medium
Walks Up to one hour a day
Grooming Every day

Extrovert and energetic, this happy-go-lucky breed thrives on human companionship, loves children and is willing to go anywhere at any time. He requires a little patience to train, but is eager to please.

 Points: 10

STAFFORDSHIRE BULL TERRIER

Size Small
Walks Up to one hour a day
Grooming Once a week

Renowned for his courage, although to his family he is kindness itself and his genuine love of children is well known.

Points: 5

Points: 20   Top Spot!

20

WELSH TERRIER

Size Medium
Walks Up to one hour a day
Grooming More than once a week

He makes a very satisfactory house dog with a love of family companionship. He is a dog with a cheerful spirit and is good with children.

WEST HIGHLAND WHITE TERRIER

Points: 5

5

Size Small
Walks Up to one hour a day
Grooming More than once a week

One of the most popular of the terrier breeds, the 'Westie' has an outgoing personality. He makes an ideal companion and playmate for youngsters as he is full of fun and virtually tireless.

i   *Westies were supposedly bred for their pure white coat which made them easier to see when they were hunting in thick undergrowth.*

Points: 15

AFFENPINSCHER

Size Small
Walks Up to one hour a day
Grooming More than once a week

Full of mischief, he is a lively little character, very affectionate, and his comical antics make him an entertaining companion.

BICHON FRISE

Size Small
Walks Up to one hour a day
Grooming Every day

A happy little dog who thrives on being the centre of attention, he is a complete extrovert, full of confidence and intelligence.

Points: 5

BOLOGNESE

Size Small
Walks Up to one hour a day
Grooming Every day

He delights in family activities and expects to be included in long walks as well as indoor or garden games.

Points: 15

Points: 5

CAVALIER KING CHARLES SPANIEL

Size Small
Walks Up to one hour a day
Grooming More than once a week

He enjoys the simple pleasures – a long country walk, meandering round the shops or sitting beside you in front of the fire. Good with children, he is a devoted companion and easy to care for.

Ronald Reagan owned a Cavalier called 'Rex' during his time in office as US President. Rex often pulled too hard on his lead and would drag the Reagans away from reporters and photographers before anyone could ask the President any questions!

CHIHUAHUA (LONG COAT)

Points: 5

Size Small
Walks Up to one hour a day
Grooming More than once a week

He is a big dog at heart, but his small size makes him easy to take anywhere. He is highly intelligent, easily trained and makes a delightful companion.

CHIHUAHUA (SMOOTH COAT)

Points: 5

Size Small
Walks Up to one hour a day
Grooming Once a week

Elderly people find him an ideal pet, happy to be a much-loved lap dog and also a good house dog, announcing the approach of strangers. However, he is not a suitable pet for small children.

CHINESE CRESTED

Size Small
Walks Up to one hour a day
Grooming Once a week

Affectionate and intelligent, with a strong constitution, they make unique and delightful companions and are good watchdogs.

Points: 10

ENGLISH TOY TERRIER (BLACK & TAN)

Size Small
Walks Up to one hour a day
Grooming Once a week

He makes a charming and intelligent companion, whose smooth, glossy coat requires minimal care.

Points: 25 Top Spot!

Points: 15

GRIFFON BRUXELLOIS

Size Small
Walks Up to one hour a day
Grooming More than once a week

This monkey-faced fearless little dog is a constant source of amusement and delight to those fortunate enough to own him. His terrier-like qualities mean that he is happy to indulge in plenty of exercise.

ITALIAN GREYHOUND

Points: 10

Size Small
Walks Up to one hour a day
Grooming Once a week

Cheerful, brave and courageous, with beautiful delicate lines, he has a gentle and loving nature. He is comfort-loving and will happily wrap himself in a blanket.

i *This breed has had some royal fans, including Mary, Queen of Scots, Catherine the Great, Queen Anne and Queen Victoria.*

Points: 10

JAPANESE CHIN

Size Small
Walks Up to one hour a day
Grooming More than once a week

Although he is a dainty little dog, he is in no way delicate. He is bright and intelligent, very stylish and extrovert and has a constant look of astonishment!

KING CHARLES SPANIEL

Top Spot! Points: 20

Size Small
Walks Up to one hour a day
Grooming More than once a week

A true aristocrat, he is elegant and cheerful, and makes a very affectionate, devoted companion, while his large, dark eyes give him a soft, appealing expression.

Points: 15

LOWCHEN (LITTLE LION DOG)

Size Small
Walks Up to one hour a day
Grooming More than once a week

Affectionate, active and playful he adapts well to city life and has many qualities that make him a very suitable and popular family pet.

MALTESE

Size Small
Walks Up to one hour a day
Grooming Every day

His temperament is merry and friendly and he is very bright and intelligent. Hidden behind his glamorous appearance is a lively little dog that is full of fun.

Points: 10

MINIATURE PINSCHER

Size Small
Walks Up to one hour a day
Grooming Once a week

He is a lively and high-spirited dog with quick reactions and a great sense of hearing, which makes him a good little guard dog.

Points: 10

PAPILLON

Points: 10

Size Small
Walks Up to one hour a day
Grooming More than once a week

He is a lively breed requiring a lot of human company. He is happy, easy to teach and train and loves activities like agility!

PEKINGESE

Size Small
Walks Up to one hour a day
Grooming Every day

Mischievous and playful, loving and sensitive, he is said to have the heart of a lion and shows this by guarding his toys and other possessions.

 Points: 10

POMERANIAN

Size Small
Walks Up to one hour a day
Grooming More than once a week

Always eager to play, he is lighthearted, active, sweet-tempered and affectionate.

Points: 10

Points: 5

Size Small
Walks Up to one hour a day
Grooming Once a week

A dignified dog, very intelligent, loves his family and is good-natured and sociable. He is robust and self-reliant, with great character and personality.

i *A Pug called 'Frank' plays an agent in the Men in Black films during which Frank turns out to be a species of alien called a Remoolian.*

YORKSHIRE TERRIER

Points: 5

Size Small
Walks Up to one hour a day
Grooming Every day

His terrier-like qualities include a hunting instinct, be it for a toy in the house or a rodent in the garden. He loves games, and appreciates a good walk.

i *As you would guess from the name, this breed comes from Yorkshire and Lancashire but is thought to have descended from a mix of breeds brought down from Scotland during the industrial revolution.*

AKITA

Size Large
Walks More than two hours a day
Grooming Once a week

Devoted and protective towards his owners, he is also very affectionate.

Points: 10

BOSTON TERRIER

Size Small
Walks Up to one hour a day
Grooming Once a week

A smart looking breed, he is good tempered and a happy house dog – if a little boisterous!

Points: 5

BULLDOG

Points: 5

Size Small
Walks Up to one hour a day
Grooming Once a week

Although this delightfully 'ugly' dog is a little bit stubborn by nature, he is good-tempered and affectionate with children.

Although this is an iconic British breed, the US Marine Corps have a Bulldog as their official mascot and many bases have their own resident Bulldog!

Points: 10

10

CHOW CHOW

Size Medium
Walks Up to one hour a day
Grooming Every day

The Chow is reserved, stand-offish and extremely loyal to his owner, with a tendency to be a one-person dog.

i *Chow Chows are distinguished by their unusual dark blue tongues.*

DALMATIAN

Points: 5

5

Size Medium
Walks More than two hours a day
Grooming Once a week

An excellent companion and house dog, he is an active, agile dog, who enjoys plenty of exercise and is more suited to country life than the town.

i *Most Dalmatian puppies are born completely white and do not begin to develop their spots until they are around two weeks old.*

FRENCH BULLDOG

Points: 5

Size Small
Walks Up to one hour a day
Grooming Once a week

A dog that enjoys his home comforts, he has a jolly and charming personality and is full of life, although he is not boisterous or noisy.

GERMAN SPITZ (KLEIN)

Size Small
Walks Up to one hour a day
Grooming Every day

An independent character with a happy outlook on life, he makes an ideal pet that is quite capable of living with old and young alike.

Points: 15

GERMAN SPITZ (MITTEL)

Size Small
Walks Up to one hour a day
Grooming Every day

He is not a difficult breed to look after but his thick coat must be groomed thoroughly to keep him tidy.

Points: 15

20 Points: 20 Top Spot!

JAPANESE SHIBA INU

Size Small
Walks Up to one hour a day
Grooming Once a week

The Shiba Inu is one of the few ancient dog breeds that still exists and he was originally bred as a hunting dog. He's a very alert, small dog, that gives the impression of being interested in everything going on around him.

JAPANESE SPITZ

Points: 15

Size Medium
Walks Up to one hour a day
Grooming Every day

A small, nimble dog that doesn't need lots of food or exercise. His affectionate nature makes him an attractive household pet who will announce visitors in a forceful manner.

Points: 15

KEESHOND

Size Medium
Walks Up to one hour a day
Grooming Every day

He will let visitors know that their arrival has been detected but will then greet them as long-lost friends! A hardy dog, he will take all the exercise you want to give him.

LHASA APSO

Points: 5

Size Small
Walks Up to one hour a day
Grooming Every day

He is of an independent nature and can be quite stubborn and wary of strangers but is very loving and affectionate to friends and family.

 This breed comes from Tibet, where they were used by monks to guard the temples – they were also believed to be reincarnated lamas (priests).

Points: 5

MINIATURE SCHNAUZER

Size Small
Walks Up to one hour a day
Grooming More than once a week

His size makes him a popular town dog. Robust, hardy and agile, he is also very alert, warning of the approach of strangers to his property.

POODLE (MINIATURE)

Size Small
Walks Up to one hour a day
Grooming Every day

A clown by nature and a born entertainer devoted to his family. He is capable of learning quickly and enjoys showing off.

Points: 10

POODLE (STANDARD)

Size Large
Walks Up to one hour a day
Grooming Every day

He is loving and loyal and will always show his appreciation when he has been given a good grooming.

Points: 10

Points: 5

POODLE (TOY)

Size Small
Walks Up to one hour a day
Grooming Every day

Light-hearted, elegant, friendly and high-spirited with a happy nature and home-loving instincts he makes the ideal companion.

SCHNAUZER

Size Medium
Walks Up to one hour a day
Grooming More than once a week

Gentle, patient and trustworthy with children, he is the ideal companion for an active person who is able to give him plenty of exercise.

Points: 15

SHAR-PEI

Size Medium
Walks Up to one hour a day
Grooming Once a week

Despite his frowning expression, the Shar-Pei is a very affectionate dog, particularly towards people.

Points: 5

SHIH TZU

Points: 5

Size Medium
Walks Up to one hour a day
Grooming Every day

He is a bouncy character and very outgoing. A complete extrovert and full of enthusiasm he makes a great companion who is happy to be part of any family.

TIBETAN SPANIEL

Size Small
Walks Up to one hour a day
Grooming More than once a week

He has a lovely temperament and can sometimes sport a snooty expression – but he is only too ready to let his hair down in a mad rush round the garden with his friends!

 Points: 15

TIBETAN TERRIER

Size Medium
Walks Up to one hour a day
Grooming Every day

The liveliest of the Tibetan breeds, he is energetic, enthusiastic and enjoys playing at being a guard dog!

Points: 15

ALASKAN MALAMUTE

Points: 5 5

Size Giant
Walks More than two hours a day
Grooming Every day

He is massively built but also dignified; this does not mean he lacks a sense of play but he sometimes doesn't know his own strength.

BERNESE MOUNTAIN DOG

Size Giant
Walks Up to one hour a day
Grooming More than once a week

Never aggressive, he is kind and courteous, well-mannered and affectionate. Obedient and easily trained, he makes a perfect companion for children and a devoted family pet.

Points: 10

BOUVIER DES FLANDRES

Size Giant
Walks Up to one hour a day
Grooming Every day

His impressive eyebrows, beard and moustache make him look fierce but he has a friendly character, is quiet in the house and is good with children.

Points: 15

Points: 5

BOXER

Size Large
Walks More than two hours a day
Grooming Once a week

A gentle, quiet Boxer does not exist; he is extrovert and energetic, loyal and fun-loving and always happy to join in noisy family games!

BULLMASTIFF

Size Large
Walks More than two hours a day
Grooming Once a week

Highly spirited, he makes a happy companion who is totally devoted to the members of his family.

DOBERMANN

Size Large
Walks More than two hours a day
Grooming Once a week

A Dobermann has a very adaptable outlook to life and fits into a family well – and will take over the most comfortable chair in the house without a second thought!

Points: 5

Points: 5

DOGUE DE BORDEAUX

Points: 5

Size Large
Walks Up to one hour a day
Grooming Once a week

Despite his large size, he is surprisingly agile and able to jump considerable heights. He makes a loyal and affectionate member of the family.

> *This breed was made famous by the film 'Turner and Hooch' where the big slobbery dog 'Hooch' was played by a Dogue de Bordeaux called Beasley.*

Points: 15

GIANT SCHNAUZER

Size Large
Walks More than two hours a day
Grooming Every day

He is slow to mature and can be rather bold, but he is trainable, a good house dog and a lovable pet.

Points: 5

GREAT DANE

Size Giant
Walks More than two hours a day
Grooming Once a week

His kind character, affection for children, devotion to his family and easy tolerance of other animals make him an excellent house dog.

'Scooby Doo' is generally believed to be a Great Dane, and was drawn for Hanna-Barbera by animator Iwao Takamoto who based his illustrations on sketches of the pet Dane of a colleague.

LEONBERGER

Points: 10

Size Giant
Walks More than two hours a day
Grooming More than once a week

A naturally powerful dog with an even temper, though not as massive as his peers.

Points: 15

MASTIFF

Size Giant
Walks Up to one hour a day
Grooming Once a week

A very intelligent dog, he is not excitable but is affectionate towards his owner and requires plenty of human contact.

NEWFOUNDLAND

PORTUGUESE WATER DOG

Size Giant
Walks Up to one hour a day
Grooming Every day

This gentle giant is eager to please and makes a very suitable companion for children, joining in their games.

Size Medium
Walks Up to one hour a day
Grooming Every day

He is a friendly dog, even if he can be self-willed. He needs firm handling when young to overcome this stubborn streak.

 Points: 10

Points: 15

Points: 5

ROTTWEILER

Size Large
Walks More than two hours a day
Grooming Once a week

Although he is strong and imposing, he is easily obedience trained and enjoys working. He has natural guarding instincts, but is not aggressive by nature.

Many Rottweilers are very vocal and quite often 'talk' to their owners by moaning and grumbling, which may be mistaken for growling.

RUSSIAN BLACK TERRIER

Points: 15

Size Large
Walks More than two hours a day
Grooming Every day

This is a dog that will stop trespassers in their tracks but despite this he is not aggressive and has a friendly nature.

ST. BERNARD

Points: 5

Size Giant
Walks Up to one hour a day
Grooming More than once a week

St. Bernards are very kind-hearted dogs and this is plain to see in his expression. Just as well, because the idea of an extremely large grumpy St. Bernard doesn't bear thinking about!

SIBERIAN HUSKY

Size Medium
Walks More than two hours a day
Grooming More than once a week

He has a delightful temperament, loves humans and never forgets a friend. His downfall is that he is a natural hunter – his prey may include the family cat or rabbit and he cannot be trusted off-lead!

Points: 10

TIBETAN MASTIFF

Size Giant
Walks Up to one hour a day
Grooming More than once a week

Owing to his heritage as a guard dog of livestock, he can be distrustful of strangers – but he is generally friendly.

Points: 15

INDEX

i-SPY

How to get your i-SPY certificate and badge

Let us know when you've become a super-spotter with 1000 points and we'll send you a special certificate and badge!

HERE'S WHAT TO DO!

- ✓ Ask an adult to check your score.

- ✓ Visit www.collins.co.uk/i-SPY to apply for your certificate. If you are under the age of 13 you will need a parent or guardian to do this.

- ✓ We'll send your certificate via email and you'll receive a brilliant badge through the post!